DEDICATION

I would like to dedicate this book to both of my children,
Savvy and Jaiden, who inspired me to write Messy Monster.
A huge thank you to my family and friends
for their love and support through this journey - both parenting, and writing my first book.

To all the parents out there that have messy children - we've got this!

Little Miss Bessie and her big brother Jessie
Were both super messy.

Bessie's toys laid all over the floor...
While Jessie's underwear hung from the door.

Their hairbrush in the tub and toothpaste on the wall,
Well they didn't mind, not even a little, not even at all!

They stormed through the house and destroyed all their things,
Her dolls and his toys all seem to grow wings.

Mama and Papa were now going crazy...
Because their young children were being so lazy.

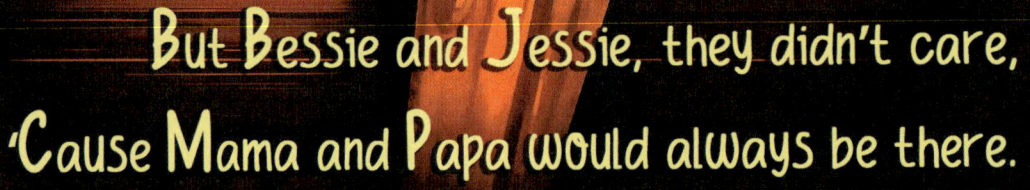

But Bessie and Jessie, they didn't care,
'Cause Mama and Papa would always be there.

They'll never stop with all of their ruckus!
So Mama cried out, "Somebody please help us!"

They laughed and they laughed, as they sat by the door,
Now Mama and Papa were ready to roar!

"Enough is enough, now you go to bed!!!", Screamed Mama and Papa while holding their heads.

They wiggled and giggled while walking to bed,
But they didn't know the creature they fed...

Outside in the storm, while the kids were now sleeping...
Two glowing blue eyes, through the window came peeping.

See you didn't know of a creature still living,

Who lurks in the dark, while children are dreaming.

As big as a door, with white silky long hair,

He didn't quite look like a stuffed Polar Bear.

Four fingers and toes, he didn't wear clothes,
And a round fuzzy belly, that could sometimes be smelly...

His cute tiny mouth made barely a peep,
So kids could continue to count all their sheep.

His round bushy tail, sucked all that's around him.
And into his belly, it went like a trash bin.

Nimble and swift and fast like a snake,
Nobody would know, nobody would wake...

He rollied and pollied all over the ground,
Till he finally stopped when something was found.
He grabbed and he gathered all toys left behind,
Cause surely he thought, these toys must be mine!

He took all the toys of naughty young children,
Who never and never would ever just listen...

Who is he you ask? Is he an imposter?

No darling sweet child,
He's the big, Messy Monster!!!

Pick up all your toys and clean all your things,
Because if you don't this creature will ring.
A lesson was learned by Bessie and Jessie,
No toys when they woke, not even Loch Nessy.

Both huffed and they puffed while they walked down the stairs,
To find both their parents with smiles in their chairs.

The house was now clean, yet the children were sad,
Cause they lost all their toys for being so bad.

"Now children, young children, quit being so grumpy."

"If you picked up your toys, you wouldn't feel all this slumpy."

"But Mama and Papa, where did they all go?"

"Sit down my young children and soon you will know."

So the story was told to Bessie and Jessie,
About a Big, Fuzzy Monster, whose nickname was "Messy".
There's no need to worry, Messy ain't all that bad,
He takes all the toys to kids who are sad.

See it breaks his big heart, when toys are mistreated,
When there are some kids whose toys are depleted.
His mission in life, to help kids change their ways,
While giving to other who have little to praise.

When you hear of the story about a monster named "Messy",
Think back to what happened to Bessie and Jessie.
Remember to smile, because he's not hostile.
He's no big mean monster or a big bad imposter.

He's a Big, Fuzzy creature who acts much like a teacher,

So when you're done playing with all the dragons you're slaying,
Be sure to clean up and you'll keep all your stuff!

The End!

Made in the USA
Columbia, SC
18 April 2021